I0652775

WHEN WORSE COMES TO WORST

by TAKANORI KIMURA

©Takanori Kimura - 1st October 2008

Edited by Hikaru Kitabayashi

INTRODUCTION

When Worse Comes to Worst had its genesis as a class project during the 1997-1998 school year. Mr. Kimura, not being finished, asked me to give him a grade on trust in a promise that he would hand in a finished piece of fiction before the end of the next school year. I agreed, though, if he didn't, I was secretly prepared to forget matters. In fact, just before finishing the 1998-1999 school year he did turn in a novella which a quick glance convinced me was a classic of the English language, in spite of the many spelling mistakes, punctuation errors and sometimes inexact grammar. Mr. Kimura couldn't see beyond the red marks on the first page or two I looked at and was firmly convinced his work was a failure. Just as many beautiful people consider themselves to be positively ugly, many talented people, perhaps most, consider themselves to be great failures. Such was the was the case here, too, and there was no arguing against it.

I kept the document I had been given, though, and also made sure I had a word processor file, which I later converted into the more ubiquitous Windows Word format. I worked on the editing of the document a bit in 2001 and finally got around to finishing a first editing of it in January of 2003. The edited document is a full 90% or more the same as the document I received, with most of the changes being small things that come with the territory of correcting the English work of a native speaker of Japanese educated exclusively in Japan. Even in its roughest form, however, the story was a remarkable achievement. I would, therefore, hope that this edition, in making it readily accessible to the average

English speaker, will present it in such a manner that the reader will feel in full its inherent beauty.

Hikaru Kitabayashi

6 October 2008

Chapter 1

In the beginning, there was a punishment, and it was named weariness. One wise man said that was an omen for the future, but destiny has been neither kind nor foolish enough to tell us whether this is so. And so, we cannot help living without fear for the future.

I am similar to a tiny lost bird searching for a safe and comfortable bird-cage in which to stay. In my childhood, I believed I would be able to change the universe. But now, I am squatting on the street in the dark of night. The street is crowded with people. I look up. There are no stars. Too many city lights are shining here and there. Some of the homeless have started coming back to their cardboard nests and I hear their rhythmical snoring. I try to sleep against a stone wall. It feels so cold. I touch the dry pavement and can feel the movements of people. Everybody assembles to keep warm next to each other.

It is early spring. I hate spring because it reminds me of the end of life. In winter, wild living things try to survive some way or other and most of them succeed. But in the early spring, just when they begin to feel happy and safe, they die, having spent all of their energy in surviving the winter. This is the season in which I smell death in its fullness. Now, I lie down on the pavement. The hard and cracked pavement is my cradle. It trembles with the passing of big cars that I can hear running by. I can also hear a lullaby. The sounds of snoring people and cars' horns make me sleepy.

I do not know when I started living here. I cannot remember anything about myself, as I have never been interested in my past. I only feel what is now. But that's all right! It's alright that I don't know my name, my age, or my hometown. If I look at my hands, though, I can see many wrinkles, so I think I am old.

I sometimes say to myself, "What if I were not a part of this world?"

Then, Mr. Weariness comes to me and invariably says, "It is nonsense to think of that."

He is my only friend. He wears a shabby corduroy jacket and a brown hunting hat. It is his custom to rub his beard. I do not know when I first met him, but he is always standing beside me.

"Oh, please, please, let me leave you," I whisper weakly with tears beginning to well up in my eyes.

Mr. Weariness sighs deeply with compassion. He touches my left hand and takes it and guides it to his hairy cheek slowly. I feel the warmth of his face and hands.

"Are you cold? Come to me. Don't be shy. I can make you warm."

I sob as my body trembles. I do not know when I got involved in the squalidness of survival. I sometimes feel pain because of my past failure. Actually, I've forgotten my past, but I have not lost that last lingering feeling of regret for my past. One day, in fact, I noticed that I felt joy in re-tasting the pain. Perhaps, I have fallen into an abyss. If so, I would not like to climb out because the process of falling involves so many questions and questions are the only things I have left which are completely mine. For instance, just how deep can I fall? Can I see the bottom of the darkness? Are darkness and light, in the end, the same?

Mr. Weariness squats to take a look at a funny sleeping face, one of the proud lords of a cardboard nest. He suddenly says without looking up, "Come on. Here is the entrance of the abyss."

He takes me by the hand into a small and dirty cardboard house. He goes into it. A couple of homeless people are snoring without noticing us.

"I'll show you the bottom of the abyss," he says.

It is damp and dirty inside. I creep into it. Suddenly I feel a sensation of falling downwards. I look up. The small entrance above me becomes smaller and smaller. All I feel is the warmth of Mr. Weariness. He keeps hold of my hand, rubbing it as we fall and pulling me ever closer to his body.

In the abyss, I cannot see anything. I do not know which way is up or down. Weariness makes me sleepy, but regret sticks in my heart. This sharp pain just barely prevents me from losing my consciousness which is all I have of my existence left, having lost everything else that would contribute to my sense of human self-worth. Only the pain of regrets testifies to my having been a human being.

"I love you," Mr. Weariness says to me in low voice.

"Don't tell something I already know," I reply.

Then, I am hugged by him, enveloped in his big arms. He smells of the cigarette smoke that clings to his shabby corduroy jacket. He tells me something, but I cannot identify what he says. My mood is calm like the little white rippling waves of water one can see on a fine and windless day.

"I can be a ship for you," Mr. Weariness says. "You are migratory bird migrating the length and breadth of the

Pacific Ocean. If you got lost from your flock, I could lend you my big arms and break your inevitable fall. When you are hungry, I could give you my flesh to eat and my blood to drink. But if the storms of life break my body into pieces, don't feel sad or sorry. Sing a song of your home town and your childhood. You must go on with your life. At least, my dear, lost bird, the screaming from my bones breaking and my guts falling out would frighten away the sea devils that make your transit so perilous. In any case, you must stay with me and find a home in my flesh. Darkness, perhaps, will prevent you from finding a compass star, but, even in death, my screaming will shine, lighting up your destination. I will never abandon you on the lonesome ocean all by yourself. You are all I have, my only beloved."

I reply sobbing like a child, "I'm so sleepy."

"Then, sleep and, as you sleep, let's fall into the abyss together."

"But if I sleep, will I continue meeting you, hugging you, feeling your heart beat and your warm cheek against mine in my dreams?"

"You know I will always be with you, because together we make up the same piece of cloth. You are the woof and I am the warp. That's why we have had so many points of contact during your life. If you ever really and truly wake up and I am not there, it will still be our destiny to meet again in some future life and that life's death."

The falling does not stop. But as I fall, for such a long time, I have the feeling that I am walking in a dream in the abyss. I have no idea of whether it is real or not. I just keep falling on and on, and am walking as I fall. Sometimes I can feel a stream of darkness passing by. The stream runs through my body and I put my hands into the stream. It is slow and soft and just a little bit chilly. It reminds me that I, too, once had nostalgic memories. It is similar to a river which one can find in the countryside of my home town.

In my childhood, I fished in that river in the early spring. The flowing water there was all so soft and chilly. Sometimes small pieces of ice would be floating down the river and I would chase them, because I wanted to know how far the ice could go in its travel to the outside world. But if I chased the ice even just a minute or two, I would find it had melted. It was gradual but, at last, it would vanish from the world. One time, I noticed there was a brown chestnut leaf in a small piece of ice. When the ice vanished, the brown leaf started floating down the river. It was a tiny leaf, but it had inherited a will to survive and the ice helped it to do so.

Now Mr. Weariness and I take our clothes off and we begin bathing in this stream of darkness. Our hair dances in the current and the nudity of our naked bodies being washed by oblivion brings me contentment.

"Cold," I utter involuntarily.

This stream sharpens my sense of having a body, a real body and not just an illusion of an existence. As Mr. Weariness and I put our clothes back on, I ask myself what would happen if my body were to vanish from the world. Who would there then be to follow this stream instead of me? A question with no answers! It is my destiny to move ever onward down to a slow death.

Suddenly, I notice a very small fire gleaming in the darkness. It is hard to identify and it is colored blue. A current in the air points me in the direction of the fire and I can see it getting bigger and bigger.

"This is a compass star and will guide us like the pole star guides sailors," Mr. Weariness says.

Now I can see it getting bigger, getting as big as the moon. It flames like the sun. One point, though, is different. It is not a dazzling body, nor does it make me hot. In fact, it makes me even colder.

"It is an assemblage of traveler's souls," Mr. Weariness explains. "They hoped to go onwards, even after losing their bodies. But they had no friends to make it possible; and so, they have come together to become a compass star to light up the destination we are destined to reach. They were abandoned, alone at the edge of the world, and left unburied. But the abandonment was mutual. They also abandoned their friends and family, too. All that was left was unlimited sorrow and regret, the fuel for a cold, clear-blue fire."

I keep silent, but Mr. Weariness continues, "It is like a tomb here, for this is not an ordinary place. Here there are no flowers offering consolation. Here there are no means by which others can search for the dead souls that make up this star. Nobody cries for them. The only current here, the only motion, is darkness. We don't need to sympathize with them, however. They chose their destination."

"Where is our destination," I inquire, getting worried little by little.

"Don't worry that we will have to find any other than this. This is our destination," Mr. Weariness says as he takes my left hand, giving me relief yet again. "And now comes the bottom."

The stream takes us forward, moving us relentlessly onward. Several hours later, it has taken us to the bottom of the abyss. I don't feel gravity. I feel like I am floating instead of standing on firm ground.

Now, I can see the face of Mr. Weariness again. It is the first time to sense a brightness in my surroundings. But it is still vague. I can see the horizon, but it seems like I can't account for anything else. Actually, it is even hard to identify where the border of the horizon is.

I finally touch the ground and I feel hard dry land. Its one distinguishing feature is the great number of small cracks one finds here and there. Then, I look up through the darkness and I see the blue compass star. It gives us a small light. Sometimes the dark streams of lost hope that flow through the abyss hide the star. From here, they look like clouds, giving the appearance of early evening.

Suddenly, I notice a small red light to the back of me. I find a tiny food stand on small wheels and smell fish stew and roast pork. I can also hear songs and absorb the nostalgia they bring. The food stand is standing on the dry land, isolated and alone by itself.

"This is our destination. Let's go up to it and take a seat." And, with these words, Mr. Weariness starts off in that direction. I then hurriedly take his right hand and follow him.

Chapter 2

This world has no mountains, hills, forests. I cannot identify where the edge of this world is, can only identify an unlimited horizon which goes on and on in its uniformity. The only distinguishing feature in this bleakness is one shabby portable food stand. The faint blue light illuminates it, complementing the reddish yellow light coming from the fires that cook the lonely stand's food. The fires of the food stand reach out to the faint blue light that comes in several big and small strings of light through the dark clouds, lighting up the dryness of the cracked land. The closest of the streams of light appears to be nearby, so I try to go there. It lights up the dry ground in the frame of a circle and I can see the slow rises and falls of dust into dust. The blue compass star remorselessly, in its star shine, encompasses these symbols of misery. I come into the light and, there, I feel like I have become a part of a big optical-fiber cable. I look up to the blue fires of the compass star so far away and I shudder from the chill.

A few moments pass and the dark clouds hide the compass star. The strings of light surrounding me become narrower and I am abandoned to this abandoned land, aware of no one but myself. Strands of light, however, are born again, here and there, at a distance and light up the grounds around the food stand. With the birth of new lights, old lights become smaller and die. The newest of these new lights starts shining on Mr. Weariness and lighting him up. Suddenly, I feel the blue light hitting me, also, on top of my head.

Mr. Weariness stands right there in front of me, beckoning me, but between him and me, the darkness runs. Even if it is only a short distance, it seems unlimited in its power to separate me from my beloved.

"Come back to me! I am a sign for you. Come back to me," Mr. Weariness shouts. "Come back to me, back to the source of tenderness and of dreams."

I cannot move, not even a little. The light freezes me like ice. I try to push my left hand out for him to reach, but I cannot do anything.

Instead, he rushes to me. He takes my hand. His warm arms and hands and chest give me back my sense of life as he hugs me tightly.

"You are too close to the dark souls of the hopeless. The compass star has fallen in love with you and wants you to join it in its orgasms of misery. I was worried for you."

Mr. Weariness spoke to me with tears in his eyes and his hairy face seems to sweat with his tears. The long and tenuous optical-fiber-cable-like lights become slowly smaller in scope until they finally disappear. After a few moments, we find ourselves standing in each other's arms on the dry ground of the darkness.

"Come with me. You now have to face a judgment and the witnesses are waiting," Mr. Weariness tells me calmly.

"A judgment? Am I to be tried? Where?"

Mr. Weariness takes his right forefinger and points to the small wooden food stand. It seems old and forbidding.

"Is the trial over there?"

Mr. Weariness nods and takes my left hand as we go to the small food stand.

A few moments later, I find myself accustomed to seeing through the twilight. A red paper lantern lights up the darkness. We part the curtains in front of the food stand's counter and take our seats. There are five green stools, each with three legs. Sitting at the counter, I can hear the sounds of boiling fish stew. The smells make me nostalgic and so, in his own way, does the master of the establishment who is sleeping as he sits in front of us. The regular rhythm of his strong snoring rids me of my worries, because it has energy and the presence of energy means I still have an existence. We sit and keep silent.

Mr. Weariness suddenly opens his mouth to say, "This is the place of anonymity. Nobody has a name. Nobody has a past. Time stops here and is blank. Take a look. There's a drunkard beside you sleeping at the counter."

"Where," I reply.

When we came here, nobody was here. But I turn to my right and I find a middle-aged man beside me asleep at the counter. He's clearly drunk too much. At the same time, I somehow think he is similar to someone I know. But I can't remember. I turn to my left and see an old fortune-telling book on the shelf.

The shabby wooden counter seems to smell of spilt alcohol.

I can feel my sweat making my corduroy jacket sleeves wet.

The food stand's low ceiling has become sooty because of the smoking of former customers. As for me, I just gaze at the boiling fish stew. The sound comforts me, as does a small, old radio playing 'Summertime'. I love that song, so I start humming. With this, the middle-aged man to my right wakes up and gazes at me for what seems like forever. Suddenly, he stands up and moves in our direction, but he slips and hits his knee on his stool.

He shouts, "Oh, of all the fucking shit-ass fuck-ups! Fuck off, you mother-fucking father-fuckers, before I fuck you!"

He then kicks his stool away and, with it, his mood completely changes.

"So, hi there! How's my old buddy," He asks me brightly. His mood is certainly cheery enough, but it looks hard for him to move his mouth quickly.

"Doing okay," I reply.

"Is this seat taken," He says, as he points to the stool, that he had been sitting on.

"Only by you," I answer diplomatically.

"Let's drink together? I've been staying here such a long time. I really want to drink with somebody."

He seats himself back at my right side and touches my shoulder happily. I can't help thinking he resembles someone I know.

"Where are you from," he asks.

"Well, mm, just a moment, ah, I think it's a small town."

I always feel embarrassed when people ask this kind of question. I can't just tell him I've forgotten.

"A small what?"

I can't answer his question. I can't do anything except keep my mouth closed.

"You know, silence is also an answer," he said, smiling at me.

His nihilistic eyes tell me he knows everything about myself. Still, I can't be sure, unless I probe him, can I?

"It's okay. I know who you are and why you are here."

"Are you my friend or acquaintance? I can't remember anything. But I can feel it. I can feel that you are a person who is close to me, maybe closer than anyone else. Please tell me if it's true. Tell me your name."

"I'm afraid I can't honor either request. It's a rule here not to ask one's real name and if you don't remember me, I'm not ready to fill you in. But I will tell you my code-name. Call me Falsehood."

The middle age man continues, saying, "Here we can be anything or anybody in the universe. It's just a matter of wishing. What do you want to be? A scholar? An artist? You just tell yourself. That's all there is to it. But you need to keep one rule. Only truth has the power to destroy this world, so we respect it. At the same time, we are afraid of it."

Mr. Weariness takes three glasses from an overhead shelf and Mr. Falsehood pours clear liquor into them. It smells strong. Mr. Falsehood looks like he's in his mid-30's. He talks about himself, but I have no idea whether his story is true or not. But his story sometimes makes us laugh and sometimes sob, and is always exciting.

As is often the case with drunkards, having drunk one third of a bottle, we talk about political or social systems enthusiastically. We have heated discussions about each of the popular ideologies. Reaching two thirds of the bottle, we talk about the love. We sometimes use vulgar words and we laugh a lot. When one or the other of us talks about a tragic love story, we sob and sympathize with each other on account of the story's hero. Now that we are working on the last one third of the battle, we are really too drunk to know what we are talking about. Neither of us know what anybody has said. I do not know how long we have been drinking. I feel so sleepy.

"Do you smell the darkness," Mr. Falsehood whispers.

"Hm, what?"

"Nothing, take a look! Here comes my close friend."

Mr. Falsehood turns his neck back to see through the darkness, while I listen to the sounds of footsteps.

Chapter 3

"Spring is the source of failure," A young guy now says in gloom as he comes through the curtains that separates us from the infinite twilight that surrounds us. He looks like he's in his 20s. His face is pale and exhausted. It is in strange contrast with that of Mr. Falsehood. Mr. Falsehood's face is red because of drinking, and he always looks fine and bright. He sometimes moves his under lip to his mustache to drink a drop of liquor. He makes us laugh and feel good with ourselves. But the young guy is indifferent to us. He just comes to us and sits on a stool next to Mr. Weariness. He moves his thin body nervously for a while. I think he, too, is similar to somebody I have known.

"Shall we drink together," Mr. Falsehood says, taking another glass for him.

"The wheel of fortune, the repetitions of failure, may they light up our destination." These words of the young guy come to my ears as a sound that is almost a whisper, a whisper which continues. "I hated to come here, but I had no other place I could go. I traveled here and there in search of other people. But it was a waste of time. This is the place for people who do not have a past or a name. People just make up a good story to console themselves, but the stories are never true."

"If you long for meeting other people, all you need to do is to make up in your mind an image of the kinds of people you want to get to know. It never fails," Mr. Falsehood says over a glass of liquor.

"That's a lie, a fat, fucking falsehood," The young guy, roused out of his whispering ways, shouts.

"Take a look. Here there are no mountains or houses," Mr. Falsehood responds. "Here, the oppressive darkness of deep twilight resides. But just try to think about a mountain. Just say to yourself 'Make me a mountain!' and, vois-la, there's a mountain."

"It won't happen, not here, not in any world I've lived in!"

"But maybe, just maybe, a long, long time ago, God said 'Let there be a mountain!', and there was this big, really mother-fucking huge, mountain. Well, God made the world that way, just opened his mouth and howled a bit. And here, we can do it just like him. Here, I'll open the curtains for you. Take a look."

I watch the young guy turn his head and I turn mine, too. A big mountain stands in the distance, so clear and, yet, so far away from here. In the darkness, it appears in shades of blue because of the compass star.

"But that's not reality! It can't be," The young guy says.

Mr. Weariness and I keep listening to their talk in silence.

"You are afraid of facing reality," The young guy says, continuing in an agitated voice.

"Go away! You're a dangerous bastard, a mischievous son-of-a-bitch sent to fuck up the magic of this world," Mr. Falsehood says with uncharacteristic anger.

I try to get the attention of the young guy, saying, "Excluding us, have you ever met anybody else here?"

"I'm afraid not," the young guy responds, sighing as he pauses. "Because..."

Mr. Falsehood interrupts him. "Because this is the only place you can call home, right? Just like him!" He takes his left forefinger and points it at me. "You, the both of you, are men without names. That's why you were invited. Nobody can come here without an invitation."

"It's a lie. I have a name, but I'd rather be too insignificant to be invited," the young guy says sarcastically before descending into heart-rending sincerity. "I don't want to hurt anybody else. Regrets pare my heart like a knife, little by little. A pebble, a little drop of water, a tiny sprout, insignificant things! Things which hurt nobody! That's me!"

"Did you hurt somebody," I ask him rather callously.

"Don't you remember?"

"How should I? I asked you."

The young guy seems embarrassed. He takes a glass of liquor to his mouth.

"But I know all about you," the young guy says.

"Why and how did you know me? I have never met you."

The young guy looks surprised for a while, but after a moment he seems to regain his sense of equilibrium.

Mr. Falsehood takes it upon himself to explain things to the young guy. "He knows nothing about himself. But don't worry! He will have to undergo a judgment soon."

The young guy turns his face to Mr. Falsehood and he nods slowly.

"What judgment," I shout as I hit the counter hard. My glass of liquor falls and breaks into pieces.

"You're going to find out soon enough," Mr. Weariness replies.

"Anyway, we should not talk about this now," Mr. Falsehood interjects. "I hate to touch on these kinds of problems. Let's drink together. We must celebrate this meeting of kindred souls, where one-night friendships take the place of one-night stands. After all, when and if the daytime comes, we'll forget each other's existences as we will later forget the daily problems we face."

"Yeah, that's right. True enough, considering who and where we are," the young guy says with uncharacteristic brightness.

"May I have your name," I ask him. "It would mean something."

He smiles and says, "Omen. Call me Mr. Omen."

Chapter 4

The master of the establishment starts humming a song. I notice now that he must have woken up sometime before. He stirs the fish stew with long chopsticks. His humming becomes louder and louder. Mr. Falsehood asks him to dip him out two pieces of radish and a piece of bean curd from the stew. He also asks him to give us some, too. However, when he tries to eat what he has been given, he finds it is too hot to eat as fast as he would like and he very nearly drops from his chopsticks the food he has put to his mouth.

"I know of a man," says Mr. Falsehood, having blown away some of the heat and now beginning to speak with his mouth full. "I know of a man who never ate without first hearing the humming of the master of this food stand. His rationale was that the ingredients used in this fish stew were too hard and too awful tasting to eat without the help of this fellow's humming and the special effect it is known to have on our stomachs. The husky, low tones of his voice help to supplement our digestive juices in breaking up the fish stew in our stomachs, thus changing it into something nutritious. If we were to try to eat any of it without listening to his song, we would have an awful stomach ache."

Mr. Falsehood laughs loudly. The master of the food stand continues to sit, placidly humming on a stool in front of us. He's wearing a white shirt and corduroy pants. He sometimes tries to clean his glasses with his apron because his glasses keep getting white due to the steam arising from the fish stew. His face is full of wrinkles. It is hard to find where his mouth, nose, or eyes are. Only the upheavings, here and there, of his face and small slits show that there are any trace of such organs.

"Welcome to the bottom of the abyss and welcome to my establishment. I am its master and that is the name I am known by because I am not you. Just call me the Master," the Master tells me, speaking to me for the first time.

Mr. Weariness, Mr. Falsehood and the young guy, Mr. Omen, nod at the same time.

"It's been such a long time I've been waiting for you. But it's all going to come to an end soon," the Master makes a short pause, then goes on, "You are a man who has no power to give anybody even small happiness. If you die, nothing will change. Think about it. The days will pass by with no change on account of your death. There will be no one who will shed tears for you."

"What's going on," I ask Mr. Weariness.

"You will receive a judgment soon." And, after he tells me this, he turns his face to the ground.

"Spring is the source of failure," Mr. Omen whispers, his voice being too small to take in clearly at first. But, getting more and more distinct, he says, "I was born in the early spring of 1922 in the far north."

Suddenly, Mr. Falsehood stands up and shouts out, "Fuck of the truth! Fuck me, if you must, but, if you start going on like this, I'll give you a hit with my fist you'll never forget."

But, breaking in, Mr. Omen stops him, starting over again, "In the beginning, there was an omen for the future. I was born in the early spring of 1922 by the northern seas. In my childhood, I hated the area in which I lived. All of us born in that God-forsaken place were forced to serve the government's war whims and other fancies. The government deprived me of the chance to wear new clothes, to eat sweets, and enjoy the trappings of happiness. We were all forced to belong to the same fishermen's cooperative, to lick the assholes of its boss and his son, the two individuals who were allowed to monopolize the sea territories we were required to fish in. When we wanted to fish, we needed to make a payment to the boss. My father just blindly obeyed. He never criticized. He didn't know how."

With this, Mr. Omen suddenly stops talking. He finishes his drink and starts pouring himself another. He sighs deeply and talks again, "Perhaps my parents forgot to give me a name. My father always called me 'You!' And so, I named myself 'Rudder' because my father steered his boat with a rudder and I came to be an expert on boats. Actually, boats were the only things I knew anything about. That's why I picked the name for myself that I did. A boring bit of information, but true enough, considering."

I can see a smile on Mr. Omen's face as he continues, "I can read, you know, but I'm afraid that I can't write worth shit. Our family lived in a shabby terraced house. It was close to the sea shore. If it was fine, I could see a big mountain in the distance, a mountain that would take two days, maybe three days, to walk to. It overlooked the sea in its majesty, warning us in its own way that the sea was too dangerous to swim in. Yes, it seemed shallow enough for the first minute or so, but then the sea's depth would suddenly change in a most extreme manner. And the water currents there were so strong that all the different types of sea currents could do there were to fight each other. It made things complicated for anyone braving those waters. Even for the fishermen having lived their whole lives off the sea, it was a dangerous place to swim in. You see, the waters there, they always look so calm. Yet, they're always ready to take a stranger in their grasp and, so, some people are drowned there every year. Such being the case, the people where I was brought up are accustomed to encountering death. And, in addition to our big mountain, we have other mountains that surround us completely. Isolation, that's the word! The fishing village I was raised in is isolated. We find it hard to meet people from other places, so people like to listen to stories about other towns. When strangers come our way, everyone wants to take them to stay at their house. Actually, the closest village is not that far away. But if we try to go there without using a train, we need to cross many mountains on foot. In the early spring, bears often come down to our village to search for food. There are many dangers to be found in the mountains surrounding us."

He stops a moment to drink a little liquor before starting up his talk again. "When I was younger, I really longed for the outside world. I hated my birthplace and liked going to the sea shore. Sometimes, I could find items drifting in from abroad. A couple of plastic bottles from Korea were my treasures. I could see words printed in Korean. I would take hold of any one of these bottles and close my eyes. I could then see the landscape of where the bottle had come from. One day, I even tried writing a letter to a future, unknown friend. I put this letter into a small brown beer bottle and I threw it into the ocean. I really longed for the outside world. But two or three months later, I found that my letter had come back to me. I found the bottle it was in buried in the sand. The sea around my home town has such complicated currents, and so kept my bottle from bringing its letter abroad. I realized that I could not reach out to the world as long as I lived in my little village and it depressed me. I picked up the bottle and I broke it with a big stone out of anger. The bottle, though, was similar to me, I thought that I was drifting in the currents and that my destination depended on the wayward waves of the sea waters where I lived."

Chapter 5

I feel my head aching intensely. I take my hands to head. I feel like I want to throw up.

"Who are you? Who is the reality of you," I ask Mr. Omen.

"I am yourself," Mr. Omen says, then pauses a bit to think before continuing. "The worth of your existence, you know, depends on you. This world of ours is a manifestation of your hope deep inside of your heart. It is a prison built by hope. Only by recognizing the truth of yourself can you break out from this world."

With this, Mr. Falsehood breaks in, saying, "Can you hear it? I can hear the sounds of people. I can see the bright lights of the big city. People walk here and there. It seems so busy."

Mr. Falsehood takes his glass of liquor and hands it to me, and I can see another world inside of it. I can see modern buildings and well-dressed people. Sometimes, the landscape trembles due to the ripples on the surface of the liquid.

"Hey, Rudder." When Mr. Omen calls out this name, the dry ground suddenly cracks, beginning right there. It keeps cracking with big sounds. The small food stand suffers a hard earthquake.

"Don't tell the truth! Otherwise, this world will break up into pieces," Mr. Falsehood shouts.

"Rudder," I reply.

"Yes! It's one of your names, isn't it," Mr. Omen says.

Mr. Falsehood, being agitated, then stands up and says, "No matter how that mischievous asshole sucks your teats, don't accept the truth!"

My heart is beginning to beat quickly, though. I am aware of so many blood vessels coursing through my face and neck and beating with an ever more intense rhythm. I start throwing up my liquor because of the severity of my sudden headache and a sense of overpowering nausea. At the same time, the ground cracks wider and the streams of darkness become a storm. That storm blows down on the fragile food stand hard. The Master rushes to me and has me lie along the line of stools. He then looks at the others and says, "Here comes a catastrophe! We need to judge him before it is too late."

As I try to stand up, Mr. Weariness stops me, opening his mouth to say "I, too, am you."

Mr. Omen repeats the same phrase. "I, too, am you."

Only for a moment, Mr. Falsehood hesitates, but he, too, opens his mouth and finally he repeats the same phrase, "I, too, am you."

The Master takes his left hand to my hairy cheek. He strokes my beard softly. Now I lie down and use his leg as a pillow.

"Spring is the source of failure," Mr. Omen starts talking. "Spring invites young people to go places with big hopes for the future. Somebody says that the future will be better than now. I believed it and waited for the future in a small town. I planned to be a good fisherman like my father was before me. But my father wanted me to go to school, to learn things, and to escape. He sent me to the navy preparatory school near the capital. As is often the case with country boys, I was charmed by the bright lights big city. So many young country bumpkins came there to make their dreams come true. I learned how to serve the government, how to drink liquor straight from the bottle with those who had been preparing to join the navy longer than me. I really missed my family but to become a great man was my dream. Every day, I learned more and more how to work on a ship and to shoot its weapons. In 1940, every young man was forced to take a test for deciding whether we would be acceptable as military fodder. It was a warm and sunny day on May 6th. I passed the test. I was glad to be able to serve my country. My father was also proud of me. I was going to fulfill his dream by belonging to the weapons section of an imperial battleship. But one day, when I was undergoing training for a virtual battle, I suffered a wound from the weaponry I was using. I made a mistake in my shooting and it set off a chain reaction of the worst type. The bullets bombed down on our section. And so, some of my friends died. I also received a bad injury in my left leg. Such being the case, I was discharged from the imperial navy, being considered unfit for duty. After that, other young guys were assigned to the battleship to take my place and the place of those who had accidentally died. When I went back to my fishing village in the north, my father was very depressed. I had not only failed him, but I had killed my fellows as a result of my failure. When I belonged to the navy, I thought my future was assured. But I missed the boat. I lost out on my future. And, worst of all, I was not even considered worth punishing because it would have taken too much time to organize a trial during the war with China and the preparations going on for war with the rest of the world. There was nothing I could do, except go back to working as a fisherman on the bay by which I had been raised. Some months later, my father told me the ship to which I had been assigned had been attacked and sank out at the sea off the coasts of Indonesia. I had survived because of my failure. I survived, instead of my comrades, because they had been better men than me. Many young guys had hope for making their way in the world. They were all gone, but my survival didn't bring me happiness. I could not help but living with unlimited regret."

I see Mr. Omen looking down at me with sympathy and love and sadness, as Mr. Falsehood takes over, saying, "Why did you tell him those things. That wasn't a good omen for the future and he might actually believe you. It's full of falsehood! Everything you said is full of falsehood."

"My friends felt they had a good future, the whole world at their feet. And they did, they finally found themselves laying themselves to sleep at the bottom of the ocean."

"Mr. Omen, you lied to him. The omen for the future lies not in half-remembered truth, but in the ignorance of young men's hearts."

Throughout Mr. Falsehood's brief tirade, Mr. Omen has kept me in his eyes. He now smiles at me as he speaks. "Do you know why you have come here?"

I am embarrassed because I really have no idea. I cannot remember any of my past on my own. I cannot remember my name mine, or even my age. I cannot remember anything even if it happened just five minutes before. I just feel like I am walking in a dream.

"Silence gives us a better answer than eloquence," Mr. Omen says. "Now, look to your back! Everything has started to vanish."

I turn around. The cracked grounds and the compass star start melting into the darkness slowly.

One or two minutes pass. There is nothing around the food stand. I feel like I am floating in the darkness. Only the food stand's red paper lantern gives off a small light for us. There is no ground and no sky. We are floating in the darkness. So many things float in the darkness here and there. The fish stew has become a floating sphere. Everyone is floating.

"Truth has broken up our world," the Master says.

Mr. Weariness now speaks, "We are free at last. We can go anywhere you want, because we are no longer shackled by the definitions of the world. We can make dreams come true. You can now become one with me and disappear forever into the darkness."

"But is this what I should really want? Is this what would best honor our love for each other," I say.

"Are you worried," Mr. Weariness replies, and I nod deeply. "Then you need your definitions, don't you? You need to be defined by the ground, the air and the ocean. But if you want these kinds of things in the abyss, you cannot help walking on the ground. You must feel the pain of walking on the ground in the head wind."

Mr. Falsehood trembles nervously, seeing that he now must start talking or forever hold his peace. "It's such a long time now, but you always longed for this world. Every day of your life you longed for it. You were afraid of the truth, because it always hurt you. It destroyed your ambitions. This world where you are now is where you will find your hope. You must receive it. But just imagine, even if we are free, do you want to be bound by definitions again? If you want them, you must receive all kinds of pains in the world, more, perhaps, than in the past. Here, nothing will hurt you. Nobody wants to. Well, okay! As you like it! Just imagine your foolish definitions."

As Mr. Falsehood ends his impassioned plea, the head of a statue made of crystal appears in the darkness. It doesn't look so big from where I am now sitting. A ring is floating around the statue, but the statue consists of only a head. It looks like a woman with no hair. There is no expression on her face. All it is doing is just floating placidly at the center of the ring and from it emanates very slightly a dark pink light.

"Is this a definition of yours," the Master asks me. "If it is," he continues, "be careful. There is gravity coming from that ring. It will bring us to it."

And, in fact, I feel the gravity from the ring and it disturbs me. To tell the truth, I was comfortable in an empty world. I don't know why I want any definition at all. I really don't want to feel the pains of the real world. This instinct, if I should call it that, is the only thing I have that holds me to my former life.

And, as I am thinking, the statue becomes bigger and bigger.

Chapter 6

A few moments pass, and we are standing on the ring. I look up at the statue. It seems so big, so like a large building. I can see the darkness through the crystal, as I try to walk around the ring. It takes 10 minutes to make a full circle. This statue is like an isolated island in the darkness.

"Why did you conceive the definitions? They're full of pain! The blankness of an empty world is your only hope, isn't it," Mr. Falsehood complains as he tries to sit, squatting on the ring.

"At least, the pains of the world are real and are not filled with falsehood," Mr. Omen says.

"Oh, fuck off! I don't need your damned definitions of the real world. I can do everything you can do in the darkness. Why do you always have to break me apart," Mr. Falsehood says angrily as he looks up at Mr. Omen and then continues his talking.

"When I was 31, I found a woman in my village. She was not so pretty. Her face had become brown and rough because of the sun and the hard wind from the sea shore. But she worked hard with me on my boat. She could lift 4 boxes full of fish at the same time. It was a waste for her to be a woman. The next winter, we had a child. I named her Naomi. I worked my fingers to the bone to support my family. But early in the spring of 1953, my father was arrested. Because my father violated the sea territories of the Soviet Union, he was sent to prison on an isolated island. As soon as the fisherman's organization knew about it, I was excluded from its membership because they were afraid of the Soviets. But I could not change my job so easily. The only thing I knew was fishing. My family moved to another place and I belonged to yet another fisherman's cooperative. I bought a used boat from the organization and ran up a big debt to pay back. My family needed clothes, food and education. I knew it. I went to work, went with my boat to sea. I had the confidence I could work it out well because I had inherited a great knowledge of fishing from my father. But the people where I was then living said that their waters weren't what they used to be. The currents of the sea had changed little by little because of strange changes in the climate elsewhere in the world. Only God knew where to find a good place to fish. I had no time to feel depressed. My family depended on me. In the winter, my daughter Naomi took my big, cracked hands to make them warm. It made me cry and gave me power. Every day, I searched for the fish. More and more I went further away from my house. Sometimes I caught some crabs, sardines and mackerels. My wife Emi sold them in the town. One snowy day, I took my boat into the sea of Japan. I saw the town I had been living in through a curtain of snow. It looked like a very small town from the sea. I was glad to see the town lights in the distance. In one of them, there was the light of my house. Suddenly, the landscape trembled because of my tears. The gulls keeping my boat company at sea with their flight always reminded me of my family. They, too, found comfort in the harbor of that small town. 'Oh, take me to my home now. Please, please tell my family, I'm fine, that I want to be back, that I want to be a source of tenderness and a dream fulfilled,' I thought. I wanted to fly back through the clouds like the gulls. 'Please take me higher and higher,' I thought. It was a grand sky, a grand ocean, and someday I would conquer it. I was sure I would be able to make my way be back to my loved ones."

With this, Mr. Falsehood seems to hesitate. He stands up and looks up to the statue. "Her face looks as cruel as the face of my destiny," he whispers. "It's my turn to take over. I, Mr. Falsehood, have a great truth to tell."

Then, in a clear voice he says "On May 28th in 1957, my wife died of a brain stroke. At that time, I had been at sea for five days. I knew what had happened some seven days after the funeral. My daughter Naomi was sent to live with a neighbor when my wife died. And, as fate would have it, that's the same day, a letter from my father reached me. It said he needed money to come back to Japan. He required so much money. Even though I still had debts to pay off for my ship, I sold it to get the money. There was no time to be sad. We needed to survive. But there were so many bills. I decided to send to my daughter to a cousin's house. And I decided to go to Tokyo. I was confident I could make a new life there. The day I went to Tokyo, Naomi cried all day. It made me sad. I hugged her so many times and left her in silence." With this, Mr. Falsehood smiles knowingly at me and asks me, "What do you think happened after my leaving?"

"You got success in Tokyo," I reply.

"No," he shakes his head. "I was put in a prison."

"Why," I enquire.

And, with this, Mr. Falsehood begins to talk again, "When I was young, I was charmed by the bright lights of the big city. It always made me feel like I would be success! But in Tokyo, so many young people were charmed by the same bright lights. And so many of them were drifters, homeless tramps, living like hoboes. Every young guy had hopes for the future. But they had no special skills, nothing that would help them get jobs. Nor did they have the looks or the imagination to sell their bodies. They just assembled at the edge of the city and talked about their dreams and ambitions, even if none of it could ever possibly come true. And this situation was the same as for me. I could not find a job, nor did I have the looks or the youth or the intelligence to successfully prostitute myself. I made it a rule to find one-day jobs, but I had no special education and no skills except my fishing skills. In more ways than one, I was like a fish out of water, flopping about on dry ground and aching for the welcoming arms of the open sea."

"So what happened to you after that," I say almost involuntarily. It is a stupid thing to say, but I can't think of anything else.

Mr. Falsehood nods his head and starts talking again, "When I realized I couldn't even sell myself, I started selling odds and ends which I would lay out on the sidewalk of a busy thoroughfare, a place where I could at least see teeming crowds of people walking past me day and night. Of course, I had no license to sell anything. I didn't know about licenses and, even if I had, I wouldn't have had the money to buy one. All I knew about was the local mob, but I didn't even have the money to pay for protection. And that was my undoing. One day, the mobster who controlled my district demanded the police do something. That evening, when I finished selling my goods, several policemen came to me. They told me I had had violated this law and that. At first, I didn't know what they were talking about. But when they took me to the police station, I realized I had been arrested just like my father must have been when he strayed into Soviet controlled territory. I was sent to a local prison where, until I was considered broken in, I was subject to beatings from the guards and was regularly raped by the other prisoners. Then, things got better or worse, I don't know. I started liking it and, when my persecutors realized that, they became bored and stopped."

"How long were you there," I ask him.

"Two and a half years," he answers in gloom.

"How was your father and daughter?"

"I don't know," he replies and keeps on talking. "When my cousin knew about my being put in prison, he was ashamed of me very much. He worried that somebody might notice my crime. Also, he hoped to free himself from the responsibility of taking care of my daughter. Then, one day a letter from him came to my jail. It said he had sent my daughter to an orphanage. I tried to mail my cousin but he had moved somewhere else. After getting out of prison, I went to the orphanage my child had been put into. But everyone working there said there was no girl fitting the description I had given them. I was depressed and, with the flow of time, my consciousness became paralyzed little by little. Finally, I lost even the ability to feel sad or depressed. I had lost everything I had, even my heart."

With that, Mr. Falsehood suddenly puts his left hand into his corduroy jacket. With it, he picks up a small bottle of whisky. For a moment, he gazes at it in happiness and drinks it with big, slurping, contented sounds. Several drops of the brown whisky run down his neck and into his clothing. He is indifferent to it and keeps on drinking it. After he finishes drinking, he breathes deeply. His breath stinks with alcohol. He takes a short rest and starts talking again. "I lost everything, but did get one thing in return."

"What," I ask.

"I got a lover. I have known her now for 10 years, maybe more. She always makes me warm in bed. She loves me anytime, anywhere. She always wears a shabby brown dress to hide her transparent skin. And whenever I meet her, I am surprised because she changes her face and body lines. But I can identify her, she has a smell that's not a smell, something special that always leads me to her. I go crazy over her big bust and her slim waist. I like to get rid of her clothes little by little. Her naked body is so wonderful! I like to stroke her body, feel her heart beat. Her skin looks almost transparent, as if I could see through it. And, it's always wet, so I kiss her, lick her crotch to get rid of the beads of sweat. After that, I kiss her small lips and her sweet, impassioned, kisses make me tipsy. And then, whenever I finish loving her, I go take a piss."

He now takes his bottle to his mouth again with a full, deliciously beautiful, smile on his face and says, "Oh, secret medicine, oblivion, please take my past memories to the ocean of the tears and drown them. Please take them to the edge of the world and throw them over, lest I remember more."

Chapter 7

Now, the gravity lessens and we are all floating on the ring. I can feel a sense of silence increasing ever so slightly. I can see the abyss through the ring. It is like a thin glass plate. I worry that it might break into pieces.

Mr. Falsehood, though, talks yet again, saying, "Sometimes, truth and falsehood are the same. I know because I forgot everything, my name, my wife and daughter, and my memories of the past, all because of a not so secret medicine." And holding a bottle of whiskey in my direction, he goes on to say, "And, if you're good, maybe I'll share it with you."

Mr. Falsehood starts walking on the ring. Suddenly, the ring starts cracking, emitting ominous sounds. Perhaps, it is these sounds which make me feel, for some reason I don't understand, compelled to speak. "You don't need to share anything with me. Your experiences are mine. After all, you are the one who told me that you are none other than myself."

As I speak, though, he begins moving away from me. I try to catch up with him and ask him why he is leaving me. I feel cold. The streams of darkness start blowing again and I begin to feel the weight of my body. I feel heavy and fall down on my knees.

"Are you okay," Mr. Falsehood says with a worried look on his face as he begins to move back in my direction, having, I think, sensed that I am in need.

"Not so good," I reply. I feel the gravity greatly and it pains me.

"My beloved, the pain you are feeling is not from the definitions. If you don't choose the definitions and rules of this world, you should be able to be and do anything you wish," Mr. Falsehood says with great sympathy, as he touches his mustache before bending down and putting his arms around my shoulders.

"Have you ever had pains in the deepest inside part of your heart," I reply.

"Yes, sometimes." And, with this, he stops and thinks.

I feel compelled to talk on. "It's true I've forgotten everything. There are no memories to make me feel regret. Yet, I feel the pain of regret. It sharpens me little by little. I'm going to vanish from the world soon. I can feel it."

The Master comes close to us and opens his mouth to say: "The ring is already cracking. That is a sure sign of your regret."

Mr. Weariness now holds my right hand tenderly in his as he says, "After you lost your past, you lived with me, your weariness. You lived the life of a homeless bum in Tokyo. You got food from trash cans. When it rained, you stayed under bridges. When you wanted to sleep, you slept on the street. You just followed your instincts. Whenever you slept on the road, you made up happy stories to console yourself in the lonely night. You could not remember why you were homeless. You also could not remember about your younger days and your wife and daughter. Your heart was no longer hurt by past failure. But you still feel the pain of the past. You like to re-taste it, because it shows you were once an ordinary person. You never feel excited or sad like you used to be. You've gotten older and older. And so, you are no longer capable of thinking about difficult things anymore.

You have become involved in your weariness and I am now your only true lover. Of course, you sometimes feel the pains of regret. It's from your own, innate, goodness, something which nothing yet has been able to destroy. You lost your memories but your goodness remains deep inside of your heart and it is this that won't allow you to forget. It sometimes gives you pains, the pains of a good heart."

The Master turns back. He seems to gaze at the bottom of the darkness. "Well, I think we've all said enough. Now you need to make a choice."

"Here comes the judgment," everyone seems to shout out at the same time.

Mr. Weariness, now holding me even closer to his body, says, "You are a lost migratory bird. You lost your friends and family. In your younger days, you thought it was possible to change the universe. But now, you've lost everything. You have been living your life so you might die in the future. That is the purpose of all life. But you're one of the lucky ones. You don't have any great memories to savor or re-taste or to hold you back. You are involved only in me, only in your weariness, and your weariness loves you."

Mr. Weariness pauses a bit, I think so that his words might sink in. He then continues, "This is the place of the many definitions. Don't you want to spare your life from more pain? You have no one who needs you, no one to live for. Do you worry that if you leave the real world completely, there will be someone somewhere whom you can leave an inheritance to in your will? Are you worried that you are going to vanish without having left behind any evidence of your having lived? Don't worry my beloved. When you die, you will die, but you will die warmed by the reality of my love."

"Don't believe he's the only one who loves you. I love you, too," Mr. Falsehood says.

"And what about me," Mr. Omen says. "I also love you."

"Be with me," everyone says.

"You must now choose or not choose your definitions," The Master says.

"My advice is to believe in your good fortune and that you will have a better future," Mr. Omen says.

"Stay with me and fuck the past. We can live in a world of dreams, just the three of us, you and me and my lover," Mr. Falsehood says, holding his liquor bottle firmly.

Mr. Weariness now takes his turn at talking to me, "Be with me and let us go to the bottom of the abyss. There you will feel no pain. Nobody will hurt you. We can go together toward the calm ocean of total extinction. It's your only remaining hope, isn't it? I know that you love to torture yourself. But you are my beloved and I am your only true lover, the only one who has always been at your side, the only one who has always loved you."

"Which one," everyone says as they try to attach themselves to my body.

Chapter 8

Now, I am facing three people and they are each myself. The Master gazes at the four of us in silence before making a decision and waving his hands much as if he were a wizard waving a wand. Suddenly, I hear a woman's voice.

"Ken!" I turn back. There is an adult woman standing on the ring with a little girl at her side. The voice is from the woman. She repeats "Ken!"

I see that this is my real name. I now realize that my parents really did give me a name.

"Daddy," the little girl says shyly. Now I realize why I called myself 'Rudder.' If I could just be another person, I thought that I could do anything. That was the reason for me to change my name and my past memories. The adult woman, my wife Emi gave me the pain of reality but, at the same time, she gave me the joy of love and life.

Mr. Weariness comments on the two female figures. There is more than a touch of bitter jealousy in his voice as he says, "They are not as important to you as I, but they have managed somehow to imprint themselves on your heart. You will never be able not to care for them, for they are the symbols of your past hopes. Now, though, that you know your real name again, it is a waste of time for you to stay here with me. You must be going."

"Yes, I must go down into the abyss by myself. I must go without you, without the others," I say to everyone's surprise, including that of even Mr. Weariness who seems to have hoped against hope I would decide to stay.

"If you exclude your definitions of the real world when you go, you can dream in the darkness but you cannot go up again to the real world," the Master says.

As I will not be intimidated any longer, I find I have things to say to all of them. "Now I can remember my family, and I can accept that I was the cause of their unhappiness and that that's my responsibility. I do not need anything anymore. My wife and daughter gave me back my real name. That's enough. Now, I shall give them my extinction. My wife is already dead, but my total extinction will eventually bring about forgetfulness on the part of my daughter, too. It is the only thing I can do for them, out of respect for the memory of my wife and out of hope for the future of my daughter."

"When you will die in the darkness, what will become of us? Who will inherit us, your friends? After all, we are the ones you have lived your life, by far the greatest part of your life, with. You will miss us, won't you," Mr. Omen says.

"Missing others is not regret. All I want now is to be eaten up little by little by the streams of darkness and vanish from the world. This is my indestructible hope," I reply.

"I think it's a case of timidity. You are just too timid to live in the real world," Somebody says to the back of me, but I don't know who. Maybe it was just the common thought of all of them, expressing itself independently of any.

"Everyone has the right to put an end to things and, when worse comes to worst, to extinguish themselves in peace. It's not a matter of not loving the three of you. It's a matter of loving my natural rights more. That's all, nothing more."

I now know how to sum it all up and say, "In the end, I am the only judge of myself and this is my judgment."

With a smile of relief on my face and a last wave of my hands, I walk now to the edge of the ring triumphant and am preparing to dive into the tornado of the abyss formed by the inviting arms of darkness. My preparations end and I dive.